First Edition 1997
Published by D.M. Design L.L.C.

Printed in Singapore

International Standard Book Number 1-890675-00-8

GUS TELLS THE TRUTH

Written and illustrated
by Donna Trapp

D.M. DESIGN L.L.C.
Trenton, MI

My name is Libby...

...and I like cherries.

I know a boy
named Gus.

Sometimes,
Gus plays tricks
on me.

One day,
Gus told me about
a cherry tree in the
woods.

Gus said that the
cherries on the tree
were as big as golf balls.

Gus was so excited
that he jumped in the
air. He wanted to take
me to the cherry tree.

I wanted to eat the cherries that were as big as golf balls so I went with Gus.

After walking for a
long time, Gus stopped
to look at a tree.

"This is not a
cherry tree!"
I said to Gus.

I wondered if Gus
was telling the truth.

I wanted Gus to hurry
and find the cherry tree.
I was hungry for those
cherries.

Gus looked
everywhere for the
cherry tree. He climbed one
tree after another trying to find it.

I could see that
something was wrong.
Gus looked very worried.

"Where is the cherry
tree?"
I asked Gus.

But Gus did not answer.
He just kept looking for
the cherry tree.

I was so hungry that
I began to cry. Gus
was not telling the truth.
He did not know where the
cherry tree was.

Just then, Gus and I
saw a large leaf on the
ground. It wiggled and
wobbled back and forth.

Suddenly,
two little legs appeared
under the leaf. Then the
leaf jumped on my hat.

Under the leaf
was a silly green frog
with a silly grin.

"Who are you?" I said
to the frog. "My name is
Gooch." he answered. "Are
you looking for a cherry tree?"

"Yes," I said.
"A tree with cherries
as big as golf balls."

"Who told you where to find the tree?" asked Gooch.

"I did," Gus said.
"But I was not telling
the truth. I really don't
know where the cherry tree is."

Then Gooch told Gus
that he should always
tell the truth.

And because Gus told
the truth, Gooch, the frog
took us to the cherry tree.

Gus and I stood in
front of the cherry tree.
We saw cherries as big as
golf balls on every branch.

Then Gus and I
picked and ate as
many cherries as
we could reach.

When we were finished picking and eating the cherries, Gus and I went home.

"I like cherries," I said
to Gus. "Mmmm, so do I,"
Gus said with a smile.
"So do I."